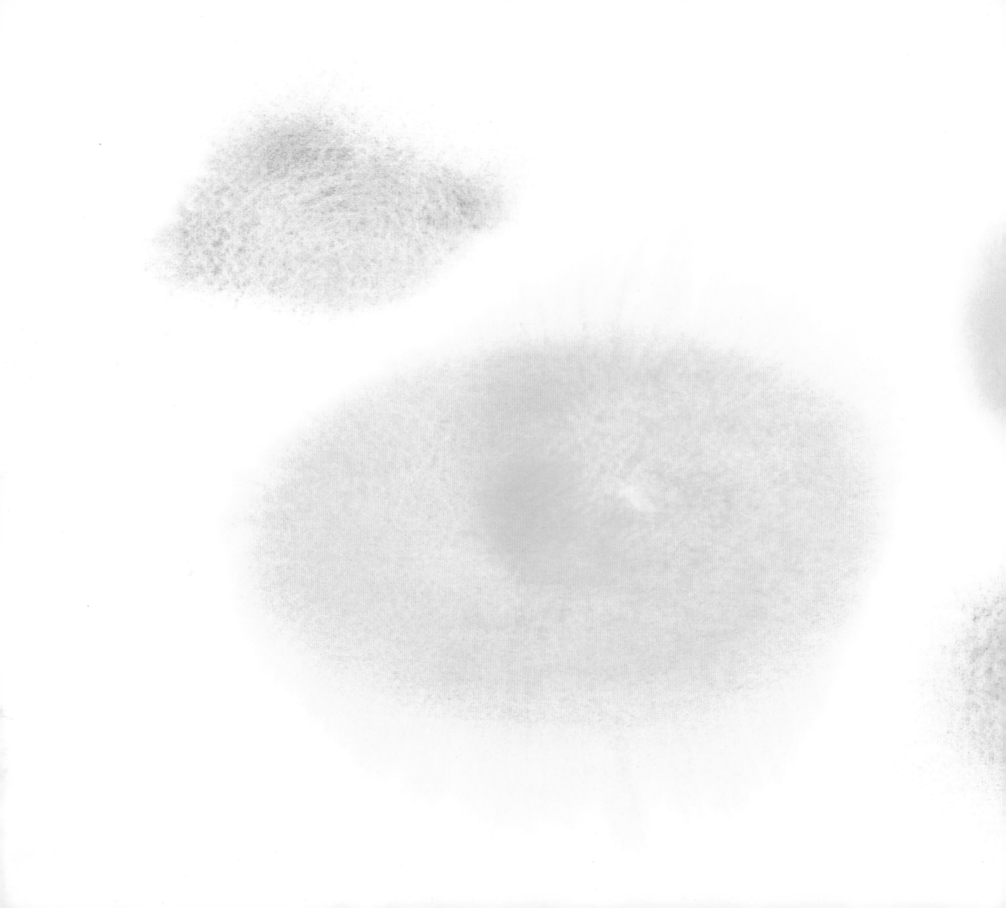

Chris Raschka

FIVE for a little one

A Richard Jackson Book   atheneum books for young readers   New York London Toronto Sydney

Smell
is

1

Noble nose,

sniff and smell.

You do it well.

Contrast,

compare.

Sample

scents

of flowers

and

foods,

oceans

and

woods.

Breathe   the air!

Hearing
is

Happy
ears,
pay
attention!

Did we mention sounds surround you?

Catch the honking,

barking,

singing.

All that ringing

will astound you.

Sight is

3

Clever eyes,

look and see.

You have the key

to **color** and **light.**

See the
sunsets,
skylines,
mountains,

sidewalks,

fountains.

Be clear, be bright.

Taste

is

4

Lucky tongue, taste and try

this berry pie.

It's a blessing!

Cabbage,  spinach,

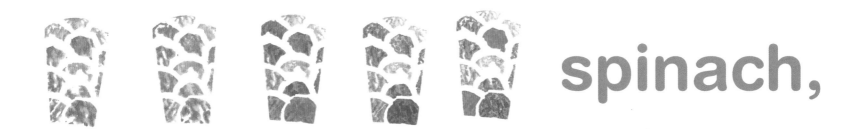

 bitter or sweet,

a joy to eat

with salad dressing.

Touch is

Playful

paws,
pounce and touch.
There is so much

for you to feel.
                    Finger feathers,

 granite,

 ice.

Wool is nice.

Make sure it's real.

FIVE
for a little one,

a little one,

who comes from two.

Five senses—just enough—to know the love we have for you.

Atheneum Books for Young Readers

An imprint of Simon & Schuster Children's Publishing Division

1230 Avenue of the Americas

New York, New York 10020

Book design by Ann Bobco

The text for this book is set in Helvetica Rounded.

The illustrations for this book are rendered in watercolor, ink, and potato prints.

Manufactured in China

10 9 8 7 6 5 4 3 2

Library of Congress Cataloging-in-Publication Data

Raschka, Christopher.

Five for a little one / Chris Raschka.—1st ed.

p. cm.

"A Richard Jackson Book."

Summary: A young rabbit explores the world using his five senses.

ISBN-13: 978-0-689-84599-4

ISBN-10: 0-689-84599-5

[1. Senses and sensation—Fiction. 2. Rabbits—Fiction. 3. Counting. 4. Stories in rhyme.]

I. Title.

PZ8.3.R1768Fi 2006

[E]—dc22 2005008963